Stun

"Wills's story is written in an extremely concise, pared-down form that condenses the effects of addiction on family, friends, relationships, jobs and education. Yet the sparseness of Wills's language is never austere or alienating—language here avoids the overblown clichés of the addiction memoir by telescoping us in on a huge stash of human emotion. Echoing the opioid epidemic that began in the late 1990s, *Stun* takes us through a world that is colder than 'the Arctic, Yukon and Mars.'"

— Peter Jaeger, author of *10,000 Hand-Drawn Questions* and *Selected Memoirs*

Praise for Stun

"Becky Wills's *Stun* is an extraordinary debut. Not so much a portrait of the addict as a meditation on humanity's flaws, desires, and truth, fragmented in the mind of a woman whose hope is eroded. *Stun*'s protagonist, Ember, proposes that maybe being lost isn't the issue, but it can—at times—be more painful to be found."

— Anthony Koranda, author of *Broken Bottles*

"*Stun* is a gripping, innovative novel about losing yourself and searching for yourself simultaneously. It's escapism that sees our deepest insecurities. Strange and poignant, this book is a goddamn treat."

— Chelsea Martin, author of *Tell Me I'm an Artist* and *Mickey*

Stun

Becky Wills

Tortoise Books

Chicago

FIRST EDITION, MARCH, 2026

Published worldwide by Tortoise Books

www.tortoisebooks.com

ISBN-13: 978-1-965199-2-99

TABLE OF CONTENTS

PART ONE: AMBER

PART TWO: EMBER

PART THREE: TRIP

PART FOUR: ONE ELEVEN POND

PART ONE: AMBER

I. ONLY CHILD

There were several lies told about why Amber was an only child.

Polycystic ovary syndrome, underactive thyroid gland, fibroid blocking a fallopian tube.

Endometriosis, the big one: a condition where tissue similar to the lining of the womb grows outside of the womb.

It's not clear what causes endometriosis, which absolved Amber's mother of much of the blame.

And a good lie lies in the simplicity. Explicitly quick, a specific shake of the mouth.

There was a common assumption: Amber was a handful.

Fitful sleep, prone to outbursts, a red-hot cry.

There was also the undeniable trouble with Amber's kidneys—technically her ureter, which had wrapped around itself into a knot of smooth muscle.

She cried until she was three years old; her blood cell count spiked white.

Rumor had it—

Amber screamed so loud in the emergency room that the ear tubes implanted after a series of infections popped right out of her head onto the linoleum floor.

Her little hands gripped crimson around the poles of the crib.

Amber screamed so hard and for so long that at a point, she stopped making noise all together.

Her mouth a big hole, transmitting at a new frequency.

A pediatric nephrologist in a bow tie made an incision on her left side seven inches wide.

Unkinked the knot, good as new.

Was there for a knock-knock joke when she woke up syrupy from the anesthesia.

But it was during the operation that they'd diagnosed the bleeding disorder, most certainly inherited from her mother.

She had a low level of a substance called von Willebrand in her blood, where the small red blood cells aren't sticky enough to attach themselves to the blood vessel walls.

She learned left and right based on the resulting lumps and bruises from the stitched wound.

It's not that having only one child was a bad thing as a general rule.

But Amber wondered why. She sat at her plastic drawing table with a pencil bag:

The tips of her hair wet from a bath as they dripped and puckered the printer paper.

Landing lights from a plane descending into O'Hare airport blinked through the window.

She began to construct a letter to her mother, endearing and oblivious:

If you have a new baby I can help take care of it.

Amber's father was in the hallway. He zipped up his suitcase, he disappeared.

Amber felt a floating sense of menace even then.

II. NEW LAWN, ILLINOIS

Amber's house was the only one on 86th Avenue dim at noon.

She laid on the Saxony carpet. It smelled of cigarette smoke deodorizer, and deep down: smoke.

Vapor rose from the manhole at the end of the block.

Directly across was the Knight family, home to seven bright blonde girls all two years apart.

Anna was the youngest. Emily, Kirsten, Meghan, Jessica, Caitlin. Samantha the eldest.

They were 26.2 miles from downtown Chicago in the shape of a backwash: south, south, then west.

A commuter train line ran directly from New Lawn into Union Station at 70mph.

If it weren't for the cement trucks and traffic cones from constant construction, there wouldn't be much traffic.

It was a tragically flat area. In one lucky spot: barely rolling grass led straight into a ditch.

A red barn even, a white wooden X over the steel garage door.

A silo caked with rust. The stench of skunk. Some hidden sloughs sporadically filled with water.

Echo Pond—the oldest living body in the town, the core source of charm.

Some gated subdivisions with names—Crystal Tree, Eagle Ridge, Arbor Pointe—where all the houses were one of four three-story models. All a ten-minute drive from a cluster of small apartment complexes, weathered brick or tornado-struck.

A wide range of Midwestern niceness—a blanket statement generally true. Always casserole for new neighbors.

Amber lived somewhere in the middle. A small kid with hair the color of ash, long and unruly.

It's true Amber wasn't terrifically easygoing—

She wasn't much interested in play. She clung to adults, in particular one kindergarten teacher with a tongue stud.

Argued while hiding her thumbs in a fist.

Not much grace: constantly spilling: tiny hoodies stained in juice.

Amber's father worked for the Food and Drug Administration in the Center for Drug Evaluation and Research and traveled Monday through Friday.

By 1999, he had acquired 753 nights in domestic Marriott stays.

Amber spent her summers in summer camp, at the aquatic center, the roller rink, a big field with softball diamonds.

She was never short of *things*—books, dolls, toys. Val bought her whatever she wanted whenever they went to Walgreens. Stationery mostly.

There was a Walgreens within a mile in every direction of Amber's house. The founders lived in a mansion just a hundred miles straight north.

A mirror just below the ceiling reflected everything happening in the drugstore.

The sunset in New Lawn was orange from pollution:

Much more beautiful than nature.

III. THE BAD BEDROOM

Amber woke up in the bad bedroom.

Which was just the state of her spirit.

It was the same physical space she always woke—one eye at a time. Vinyl blinds cut the sun in half.

Her ruby walls bled more red than pink.

At the end of the ranch hallway was Amber's mom and Gabe.

The three of them had a game: Never say Gabe's name when he's not there.

That one rule.

Amber didn't understand French but she understood that was why it was being spoken.

Valérie hung heavy in the air, expanded and snapped like a rubberband.

Gabe pronounced it accurately in his Québécois accent: *Vah-leh-REE.*

The screen door creaked and shut. He took a puff of cigarette smoke with him.

I love you to bits, Val. That's what he says to me.

Amber's mom told her at the kitchen table very pleased.

On the front lawn, dew drizzled over the grass. Amber sneezed once into the crease of her sleeve.

Her heart hammered in her head.

Val was a terrible driver. Amber couldn't as much tell as she could sense it.

Clinically dreamy, Gabe would say. But that was all too romantic.

After four hours at the local mall, endless hours of Amber watching her mother try on a series of outfits in a fitting room, Val would realize in the parking lot she'd left her car keys inside.

The problem was they'd have closed down the mall.

All of Val's purse would be emptied out by the curb stop: wallet, sunglasses, empty Marlboro Menthol packs, little coin purse, loose coins, lipstick, metal bracelet charms.

Eye shadow, eyeliner, mascara, concealer, fake eyelashes, eyelash glue, fake nails, nail file.

Chocolate bar for pick-me-up emergencies, ripped up receipts, scratched-off Lotto tickets, nicotine gum.

She'd bang on the outside of the revolving doors hoping a security guard would hear:

Shit la merde!

School mornings Amber would swing her bookbag in the backseat first, climb into the red Ford Taurus.

On the drive through the sun's tantrum she thought of nothing in particular.

The main entrance faced north. The east entrance was the carpool lane. Amber was not only determined to memorize this, but to understand it.

Teachers filed along the pavement in their designated quadrant.

Amber believed—really believed—having a good day at school hinged on whether or not she could outrun four quadrants in one breath.

Sun rays reflected off the social worker's lanyard. The day was sick bright.

Do you want to skip school today?

Val was already passing up the staff; the day was punctured.

Come with me to the mall?

The slowing of light: a rupture.

Gasoline spilled out of Val's car in the circle drive and left a rainbow trail.

IV. STUN

At the mall Amber felt a surge of excitement at the sight of a gumball machine outside the pizza shop.

Val pulled a quarter from her purse, blew off some debris.

She placed the quarter in Amber's palm held out modestly and damp with sweat.

The head of the gumball machine was three-quarters full and twice Amber's size.

She crossed her fingers for blue raspberry, watched the rainbow pile cave into itself as one gumball released.

White hit down in a spiral against the plastic slope.

Just wait a second here Amber—

Val whispered with intent.

Behind her was a boy around Amber's age. He put in a quarter and down tumbled a blue gumball.

Val asked the boy if he'd trade the white for the blue. She kneeled down to his height:

White's the best 'cause it's all of the colors at once.

Before the boy knew it, Val had them swapped.

She cracked the gumball between her teeth and handed it to Amber.

The soft sticky sugar flooded Amber's mouth and stained her tongue.

The two were halfway to a fitting room in Forever 21.

Val's pregnancy with Amber had been the best time in her life.

She took her prenatal vitamins and gained 102 pounds.

The rest of Val's family was still in Montreal. She'd met Amber's father in Toronto the year before.

They'd rung up considerable international call bills over the course of several months until Val moved in with Amber's father in their satellite village of Chicago.

That same year was the discovery of the active ingredient in the translucent liquid now labeled Stun.

It worked uniquely in that it enhanced the effects of naturally occurring chemicals like norepinephrine in the brain.

But by simultaneously activating an area of nerve cells that block pain signals between the brain and the body, it boosted feelings of pleasure in pretty much everyone.

There was little to no hangover from the drug.

The only thing anyone had to worry about was running out.

On a scheduled day in July, Amber had been removed from Val—their bodies thrashing.

Amber inhaled amniotic fluid, choked. Went bloated and blue, tubed.

She stayed in the incubator for an entire week—in the quiet fury of breathing.

Time did not stop. Matter transferred, then bent.

Where the air moved, Val went pallid and florid:

Rounding back down to zero.

V. BLUE

Every drawer in Val's dresser couldn't close. All from one loose blouse.

Val's room was directly across the hall from Amber's, only slightly bigger.

The queen-sized bed had a gold metal frame that came together in an arch up against the back wall.

The comforter: beige with a red floral pattern lined in midnight black. The walls a pale taupe.

To the left of the bed was a wooden nightstand.

On top, one digital alarm clock and a transparent bottle of powder-blue pills.

In the corner, a box TV set with an antenna, on a cupboard with a broken latch.

By Val's feet, Amber read a book about an American Girl Doll:

Val laid as motionless as the title on the cover.

What's your favorite color? Amber asked Val.

Met with silence, a shift in the air between them. The air grew tight: *Is it blue?*

Val's jaw hung by an invisible thread. Her fake front teeth ghost white.

Almost everything about Val's appearance seemed to be fake, or didn't quite match the photos from her twenties: the shape of her four front teeth with little calcium deposits and a uniform overlap, a missing birthmark on her left cheek, now her chin without a cleft.

Val tried to erase any trace of a canine-tooth smirk and a bite-marked life.

Mom...

...did you say it was blue?

Val's veins popped out of her neck like a trail of hills: the night sealed the room.

Bubbles of spit fell hard on the pillowcase. She made a gurgling sound, went dark blue.

Her nose bled too, like paint on the petals of the flowers on the bed.

Time was sharp. Time shredded out a piece of Amber.

She watched her mom's hands shake next to her knees. Amber's hands shook.

The book shook. The book fell off the bed.

No, my dad's not home. Neither is Gabe. She had broken the rule. *I'm eight!*

She was on the phone with 911—couldn't remember where she learned.

The phone had a cord that reached all the way to the bed.

She takes medicine.

She says it's to be a better person.

Yes, they're blue—just hurry. When the Paramedics arrived—

Val's head jerked violently like a curse. A burst of flashing color—then lost. Amber pursed her lips.

Outside the greater world went dim and thick.

VI. ECHO POND

Amber developed a particularly active mind.

When Amber's father's job didn't have him traveling, the two of them would walk to the pond at the end of Echo Road.

They'd reach the stop sign and her mind would force itself to take the letters of *STOP* and build them in cursive backwards.

The tracing was a survival skill—

Amber had a lot of these. Her brain found something to fill it before it filled itself.

As the two approached the pond, frogs the size of softballs jumped off the muck and back into the water.

They couldn't see the frogs, only hear the splash. *Did you see where it came from?*

No, did you?

They'd scan the edges covered in lilies. Any evidence of the frogs would often be settled.

Sitting on a bench they'd try to name the colors of the ripples: lapis blue, cerulean, sapphire.

Echo Pond was home to a gigantic tortoise Amber named Ruben, Ruby for short.

She'd imagined he'd lived there for thousands and thousands of years and had a slow wrinkled life half in the dirt.

Life is short, people would say, but it's mostly, of course, very long.

It'd be awful to be alive for all that time. Amber was actually thinking these things.

Hanging over the pond was a summer flurry of cottonwood.

Until winter hit that year all at once, and there was a real flurry, and Amber's world folded into an origami chatterbox.

There were only pockets of truth, and the whole thing seemed a game.

Amber and her dad hardly ever spoke about Val.

She knew better than to bring it up: Bringing up Mom makes Dad mad.

The headlines that year: *It's Official, Chicago Is Colder Than Parts Of The Arctic, Yukon, And Mars.*

The moisture inside her nose froze and every inhale felt like breathing through glue.

Amber slipped on the ice one day on the way back home and scraped her kneecap.

Her dad plopped her on top of the bathroom counter and put mercurochrome on her knee in the shape of a smiley face.

Someone might come and ask you some questions...

...but you need to tell them that you feel safe at home.

OK?

One eye of the smiley into a wink.

VII. AMBER TURNS NINE

Amber began to view her life from the ceiling.

All of the Knight girls' hair turned slime green from the chlorine of their unheated above-ground pool.

Amber went over to swim for her ninth birthday.

When's your birthday, Emily? She didn't realize—

She wanted to ask the question just so someone would ask it back.

Amber picked a sliver out of her heel, her skin the color of skim milk.

A Knight cousin was over. A little boy with a buzzed haircut, his lips slippery from a sucker.

Meghan said *Watch this* and kissed the boy on the mouth.

The boy took the kiss as if it hadn't been the first time:

His hand gripped vermillion around the sucker.

It looked as peculiar as seeing her mother kiss Gabe. The wet click of their tongues—

And Meghan eating chips like she was in an audience.

Amber did not realize that the feeling of her face going hot might be visible to other people.

They all moved inside with pruned hands to play a game of Hide-and-seek.

Anna, Emily, Kirsten, Meghan, Jessica, Caitlin, and Samantha all hid in the same coat closet in the foyer.

Kirsten held Anna in her arms. Meghan held onto the knob to make it seem locked.

Amber could hear their hot red breath and the brushing of windbreakers.

She tried to open the closet with all her might, her bare feet in line with the crack of air underneath the closet door.

Meghan's grip let just enough—

The door rushed open at the perfect angle to pop off Amber's toenail in one perfect piece and slice open her ankle.

Amber's disorder made the blood gush. Made the gash look worse than it was.

Still all the girls scattered off through different hallways like ants.

Amber was mesmerized by the exposed nail bed: the vulnerable flaked flesh bumps.

She hobbled over across the street back to Val, who was sitting on the floor in the living room.

On the coffee table was a close-up mirror.

Val was gluing on fake eyelashes as a cigarette smoked itself in the ashtray.

You're tracking blood all over the carpet, Amber. Come on, let's go to urgent care.

Does it hurt?

It didn't. Amber could see her ankle and her foot. The ankle and foot belonged to her. She factually knew they were attached.

She thought about how nice it was that her body was protecting herself from such pain.

On the exam table at urgent care, the sheer white paper crunched.

A small-boned woman with glasses took Amber's vitals while another nurse put pressure on her foot to stop the blood.

I'm afraid you'll need a few stitches and—

Honey, does it hurt? The one nurse's fingertips were warm on Amber's beating wrist.

Gosh, Mom, she's so calm—

Yes, she's used to being at the doctors. You know, I have an appointment soon, but while I'm here...

...I'm actually out of my prescription of Stun. Is there any way...

Amber had an overwhelming desire to kiss the nurse.

...that someone might be able to fill that for me?

You know, since I'm here?

Amber pushed the thought out, traced *Pain Scale* backwards in cursive.

VIII. AUTOBIOGRAPHY

A freak heat wave hit Chicago.

Amber watched a swarm of flies in the shape of a phantom near the trees.

The world was airless—she escaped inside.

She heard the zip of a suitcase and the swift clink of keys off glass.

FDA conference in Seattle. Back Friday. There's $20 on the kitchen table.

Amber leaned her face up against the screen door to watch her father leave.

Mesh imprinted on the tip of her nose.

Val locked herself in her bedroom. Not quite like a haven—

More like an inferno.

Amber began writing her autobiography.

The Knight girls gifted her a plain white hardcover book: blank blank blank.

She outlined ten chapters, one for each year of her dense life.

Was it a quiet life? Not exactly, she thought, though there were long periods of silence.

She took a break from Chapter Five: 236 words on how she learned to tie her shoes.

She waited for AOL to dial up—the sound of Martians, she imagined—not not sinister.

An instant message popped up from DaBearsRule93: *I heard ur mom is a pillhead.*

Then: *My mom said she saw ur mom in a ditch last week.*

Amber opened up a link to the online police blotter and a mugshot:

Val's face like a slurred word.

Amber clicked *Sign Out* and *Yes, I'm sure* needle-prick quick.

Val could not seem to go from point A to point B without a pound and a lash.

When she first came to America, she'd decided she'd cut hair. In beauty school they'd practice on dummies and grab the dummies by the nose to move them around.

On her first day with a real person, she grabbed them by the nose. Fired.

She got a job at a dry cleaners. She burned a hole in a $600 tailored suit smoking a cigarette in the back. Fired.

Then she made a fake resume and got an office job—

But she couldn't produce a high school diploma and they formally rescinded the offer, citing her lie.

English wasn't her first language but she always used the expressions:

I should be in sales. I could sell a cooler to an Eskimo.

She'd tell Gabe: *I can get Stun from any doctor around here.*

Amber printed out the first half of her autobiography and glued the pages into her blank book.

The night cooled and thinned with twilight.

She practiced her signature on the title page and imagined it would one day be her autograph.

But Amber didn't quite like the look of the big *A*.

IX. VAL SEES A THIRD NEW DOCTOR IN A WEEK

Val walked into the exam room and ripped up the Pain Scale.

She pinched her right suboccipital and her eyebrows collapsed into a wrinkle. Inconsolable.

I can't give you a measurement of how I feel, Val pleaded.

How do you feel?

She drew a blank. She curved into an ache. It wasn't just a performance—

The pain was really there, biting a burnt nerve root. Gripping slick halo-white cartilage. Burning a spur of precise white bone.

How the pain got there is complicated—self-inflicted.

Take Stun when you don't need it and run out abruptly: superficial pain hyperextends into your tissue bed.

Flex-swirls and rotates crunch. Fills a synovial fluid capsule and swells a masseter.

The doctor was drinking something steaming from a mug that said *GET IN THE SWING WITH STUN!*

She couldn't make eye contact. There was something unique about his mouth—

Val was distracted, painless for a split moment. Instead of two front teeth, he had one dead-center.

What you might be experiencing is something called breakthrough pain.

Just a flare up. I'll write you a prescription for a higher dose.

Val took the holographic piece of paper. She picked up the shredded faces from the Pain Scale off the exam room floor without bending her knees. Some loose tobacco fell out from her purse.

She drove to Walgreens sucking on the inside of her cheeks.

The oil-change light went on, then a little yellow wrench. The gas fuel gauge lowered below the E.

Val fixed her hair extensions in the angled ceiling mirror at Walgreens.

Wiped some smeared eyeliner, her mouth in the shape of an O.

She handed the script to the pharmacy technician—felt her mouth scrunch to the width of her nose, the way it did when she told a lie.

Val waited the twelve minutes it took for her Stun to be filled. Scratched the fabric of her chair.

She'd go through the month's bottle in less than a week.

Already the whole pointless charade seeped out the heels of her feet.

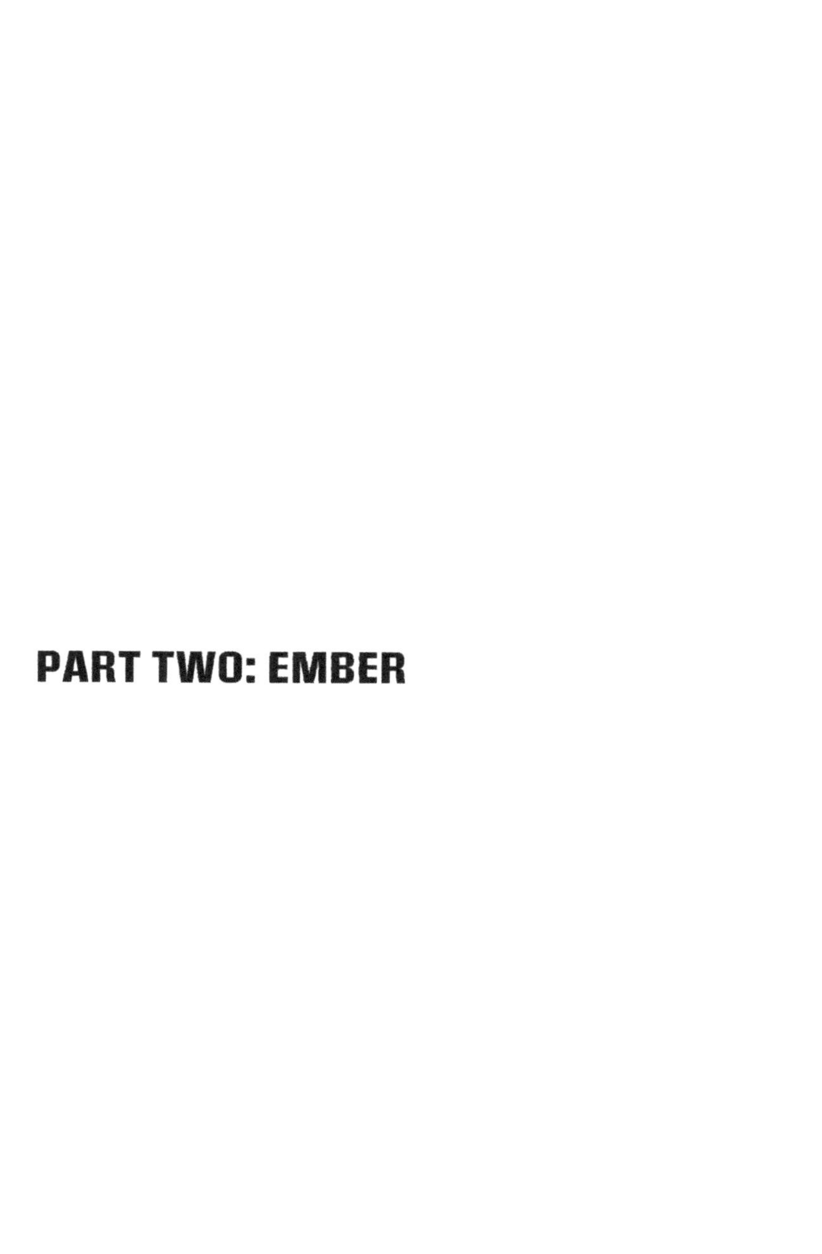

PART TWO: EMBER

X. COLOR ME NEW

Val's retina detached and she went temporarily blind in her right eye.

A thin layer of tissue slowly pulled away from the blood vessel on the back of the eyeball.

Her vision blurred. Belts of light. Then a dark licorice curtain.

The air in the house pleated.

Ember—her new name, much better for signatures—was convinced Val had somehow detached her own retina. It seemed she was in constant need of a complication—

She clung to an ailment and seemed to use it as an excuse to limit herself.

She felt incapable, so then she acted incapable, and then she was incapable:

It was all fundamentally circular.

Ember's father gave Val an allowance of $150 per week for food, gas, cigarettes. The rest she spent at Walgreens and a resale shop called Color Me New.

Val never went out socially but still she never repeated an outfit.

She would slink around in a secondhand dress like a velvet housecat.

Ember, let's go out shopping...

...OK?

Come with me.

Ember did not challenge Val driving—

Part of her even hoped for a crash—a consequence.

It'd take Ember until adulthood to realize that Val's punishment for being Val was being Val.

They both ignored the deep knocking of the Ford Taurus engine.

Ember willed the car to lean left over the ticks of yellow lane lines by slanting her head in that direction.

The village of New Lawn was becoming a sprawling parking lot of strip malls.

The musty smell of Color Me New. The noise of color-coded racks.

The owner moved around the shop like a pinball, re-organizing and rehanging aged blouses in their right place.

She flipped the neon sign in the window to *CLOSED* just as Val carried a new pile to the dressing room, reckless.

The woman untwisted the kinked phone cord next to the register.

Yes, I just have one customer left.

She looks like something the cat dragged in.

And either doesn't notice she's dragging my nice clothes all over the floor...

...or maybe doesn't care.

I won't be home until ten at this rate.

Ember was hiding behind a pair of corduroy pants, trembling with agitation.

Felt a desire to rip the skin off the night.

Ember tried to hurry Val but Val could not be hurried.

Sorry, but we closed 30 minutes ago and I'm afraid...

...I'm going to have to lock up.

Val snapped back. *I'm just finishing up! I'm getting something for my daughter!*

But Ember never took up Val's offer to buy her a new top or skirt.

She thought, if she never accepted, she might be able to prove she didn't need anything.

Eventually at home—

Val draped herself in a new outfit.

Crushed up two Stun pills in a small piece of toilet paper and parachuted the powder.

Sat defeated in the family room while she waited for the single ply to unravel in her stomach.

She ushered Ember over in French to look at her wedding album.

In the photos Ember noticed Val's maid of honor and bridesmaids were all Ember's father's sisters and his brother's wives. Not a single friend or family member of her own.

Val began to cry:

A fake eyelash dangling in front of her eye.

XI. EMBER'S MOM'S MOM

The air conditioner at Ember's blew a fuse.

To make matters worse, Val's mom was in town and Ember couldn't quite seem to call her *Grandma*.

They put her suitcases in the back laundry room at the very end of the long ranch hallway. Gave her a vanity set and an ashtray.

She kept her heavy-duty Ziploc bag full of cigarettes in the freezer.

Ember counted an even two hundred while admiring how the filters crystallized from the frost.

The fridge was full of rotten produce. Val often had one day a month where she was determined to turn her life around—

The baby spinach and crowns of broccoli and asparagus tips never did get cooked.

Val would make calls to Canada every so often to speak to her mother.

Ember memorized the sound of the specific combination of numbers being pressed into the phone and would breathe in sharply: 1-514-198-2983.

She knew by then: Val's mom makes Val sad.

When the sky turned ink black, and the house rocked asleep, Ember took a pair of scissors to Val's mom's clothes.

First she made a jagged cut in the elbows of two polyester blouses.

Then a pair of her slacks, a slash right in the left knee.

In the morning, Val and her mother discovered the ruined clothes and confronted Ember:

Ember, why did you do this? Answer me right now.

The clothes were cut. Ember cut them. Ember could not seem to connect these two facts.

She certainly did not have the language to explain.

Honey—are you OK?

Val moved in sympathetically but rushed, stepped near Ember as if to watch her pull back—

See, when I go near her she recoils! She rejects me!

C'est tout fucké!

The air fell very thin. And Ember stood very still.

When the two stopped speaking English altogether, she retreated to her bedroom.

She measured how strong she was by what time she went to sleep.

Forced herself awake in the sable black of the night.

Her breath stuck in her chest, a sharp knot growing at the top of her skull:

Ember's eyelids fighting and fluttering.

XII. CHARLOTTE

Somehow Ember made it to seventeen before she leaped into Charlotte's life.

Echo Pond had frozen over and the big metal gates opened up so the adjacent brick structure could act as a warming shelter for ice skaters.

Ember had a job there making hot chocolate and cappuccinos. At the end of the shift, she'd run a cleaning solution through the espresso machine, wash out the milk frothers, brush off coffee grounds hidden under the espresso bean grinder.

Her coworker Hunter would say:

You shouldn't be doing that on your own. Iris should be helping.

I'm just trying to finish up.

I have an extra Stun here if you want one.

For how much? Well—no thanks. I don't really take anything.

Ember was always just a little curious.

She had to show some sort of interest in the pill, or else people might assume it hadn't made an impact in her life.

But she had to show an aversion to it, to show how it had emptied her.

It was a Thursday that Charlotte first came in to buy hot chocolate. Her hair dyed the color of pennies, a sunken scar under her mouth. A crease in her skin mapped the scar to her lips.

Ember was drawn to the rolling and boxcar scars on her cheeks. She thought Charlotte looked *real*, and lived.

A cold blush sunspot under her left eye. Light-blue eyes? Topaz, maybe? Ember couldn't make eye contact long enough to name.

Charlotte could barely move her mouth from the freezing temperature. Ember knew that feeling in her cheeks, like Novocain.

Why did you move to Chicago?

Charlotte answered with a different kind of twang: *To get out of Pennsylvania.*

As the temperature lifted, she came to the warming shelter with increased frequency.

Ember's days off from the warming shelter started to feel acutely blank.

Her senses were always heightened in Charlotte's company:

Her love for Charlotte became potent.

She would trace bold figure-8s in her gloved palms to calm herself as her heart beat seeing Charlotte walk down the Echo path.

She'd have another question ready to ask her. She'd rehearse how to make them sound natural.

Ember wanted to know everything about Charlotte's life before they'd met:

A full sunburned portrait.

XIII. BEACH DAY

Charlotte left Ember disarmed.

In the summer, the building near Echo Pond became a cafe with fresh-baked blueberry scones and watermelon gelato.

Ember smoked a cigarette on the path heading into her shift.

There was Charlotte in the park: sage-green botanical-patterned dress, flat cage sandals, no jewelry.

You know, my mother used to say a lady never walks and smokes at the same time.

Well, my mother once burned her bangs off lighting a cigarette on the stove.

Charlotte covered her mouth when she laughed as she always did in the winter—

But by then it was all the bones of July and the space between them was muggy.

What do you do on your days off?

I'll probably take myself to the Indiana Dunes while Jerry is out of town...

...want to join?

I would really really really like to join.

That's three reallys.

Ember's brain filled itself with a list of things that could possibly go wrong in between this day and the beach day.

The whole world was reduced to a five-day span of calendar:

In one square she existed in the present. At the end of the week was a square with her and Charlotte at the beach. There were three empty squares in between she'd need to sludge through.

A headache would compromise the integrity of the day, but not debilitate her entirely.

She'd have to stay home if she had a stomach virus.

What if something came up for Charlotte?

In these red moments she considered trying Stun. But she sensed it'd be the start of something relentless. Best not to activate the gene.

The beach day arrived in spades.

Charlotte stopped to get gas in Indiana on the way. The headlines that summer: *Chicago Gas Prices Creep Up To Or Pass $5.*

Ember hung her head out the window to watch, her cheek in the crease of her elbow.

Their heels dug in the sand, keeping them steady on the hill towards the lake.

Charlotte packed a cooler with shortbread cookies, prosciutto, a six-inch sandwich with salami, mozzarella, olives on ciabatta, four cans of flavored La Croix.

An umbrella, two foldable beach chairs, a thin mandala print blanket.

It's like going to the beach with your mom, isn't it?

Well, not my *mom.*

Charlotte removed her shirt and skirt, sat with her back facing the water.

As the sun moved, they rotated counterclockwise, and by the time the sun was close to setting and they were facing forward, all of their things were spread out within a ten-foot radius.

Ember and Charlotte passed the salami sandwich back and forth.

Ember never shared food with anybody, but she'd deemed Charlotte safe.

She counted the bites Charlotte took: one, two, three-and-a-half. Then Ember would take one less.

The pair never went in the water together.

As much as she wanted to watch Charlotte in the water, she wouldn't let herself. She waited until she saw in her peripherals Charlotte was approaching their spot.

Charlotte sat back and let the sun bleed onto her freckled chest.

XIV. CHARLOTTE'S HOUSE

Ember always had a hard time leaving people.

On the drive back into the city on I-94, Ember wanted to talk about how they'd separate at the end of the day.

They'd been together for a full ten hours and she wanted to be sure they'd ease out of it—

Then Charlotte announced: *I'm going to beeline it to the bathroom and sit on the balcony...*

...you're welcome to join me.

Charlotte's house was evolved: high ceilings with walls decorated in large-format photographs taken by her brother. It was a series from Red Hill Island in the south part of the Luleå archipelago—35mm, black-and-white, the prints signed and numbered in the bottom right corner.

Charlotte came up behind Ember looking at 'Last Pale Light in the West II.'

They are all printed on cotton paper so you can really see the grit.

Ember wanted to soften into Charlotte.

She felt like if she didn't make it easier for someone to love her, then they wouldn't love her at all.

On Charlotte's fern-green and overgrown porch, she opened an orange prescription bottle and swallowed a blue pill dry.

Do you want one?

Ember blinked hard.

I had an accident last year so I get it because of the pain.

I see.

I've been a bit afraid because it's been a problem for my mom...

...but I get that it may not be a problem for everybody.

Charlotte cracked the pill in half and placed it in between Ember's lips.

Then Ember and Charlotte were twirling by the couch and then they were down a long hallway with six closed doors and then it was midnight.

Charlotte fell into the wall and collapsed into the hardwood floor in her and Jerry's sterile white bedroom.

Ember went over and sat facing Charlotte on her lap and they stared at each for three beats.

The air between them was dense.

I sense something in you... Charlotte said.

...we're both the cat, in a cat-and-mouse game.

And what about Jerry?

Jerry has no interest in playing either mouse or cat, so it becomes a moot point.

Ember pulled up her shirt and Charlotte traced the scar on Ember's side.

And then Charlotte told her, *Come for me.*

Charlotte's mouth shook and the night put the two of them to bed.

You're going to sleep with me in my bed, Charlotte said—

Which was half a statement and half a question and totally a marvel.

Ember couldn't come up with a response and climbed in.

Ember wore Charlotte in black lace—

Charlotte wore a blanket that turned into stone.

XV. CHARLOTTE'S SLEEP PARALYSIS

In the morning Charlotte was in a different medium.

Her friendliest cat pawed her awake and she mumbled *Hi* to Patch in a way Ember had never heard her speak.

It took Ember a few seconds to realize where she was. She pawed at Charlotte, rubbed her arm up and down.

The hot white light from outside seeped into the room and she could see fuzz floating above the bed from the light hitting just right.

Ember's eyes felt like knives.

Pinching the bridge of her nose she asked Charlotte, *Did it happen last night, the thing?*

Yes, it did for a few long minutes.

What does it feel like?

Like there's someone in the room or on the edge of the bed and then you feel like you're suffocating and can't get the blanket off or run or anything.

Ember had always associated sleep conditions, like sleep paralysis, with a brilliant mind.

She thought of the word *sacrifice*.

You *sacrifice* good sleep but you get to have a *sacred* experience.

Now things were different. Now Ember not only wondered how it felt to be with Charlotte, but knew.

The fantasy wore thin and the world moved.

Ember clung to the night like a survival skill.

The two of them were asterisks in the bed.

There was no adjustment period or thought process: She didn't need Charlotte and then she did.

Ember closed her eyes and fell back asleep for an undetermined amount of time.

She woke up to Charlotte walking up and down the hallway in flip-flops with a watering can.

Charlotte's phone was wedged between her shoulder and her jawline while she switched over the watering can to her other hand, the strap of her sundress loose, her sun-splotched bare shoulders uneven.

Ember was sure she was speaking to Jerry—

She shut herself in Charlotte's bathroom and gargled mouthwash down with force.

When she came out, Charlotte was on the other end of the hallway, slightly out of view. Ember walked past the six closed doors and the space slumped in between them.

Jerry said he's sharing a room with five people at his family reunion! Can you imagine?

Can we talk about us?

Nothing to say. Come on, I'll take you home.

Charlotte grabbed Ember's waist and pecked her quick with heavy lips.

The left turning signal was on the entire time they were on the highway back to Ember's.

Charlotte didn't seem to notice; the clouds curled flint gray.

Did you hear about the pond?

Click click / click click. Ember put words to the rhythm of the clicks: Ec-ho / ec-ho

She could see the crease in between her eyes in the side view mirror from her bulky frown muscle.

Ember must have been frowning into a headache all night—tried to iron it out with her pointer finger.

Well it's slowly been filling with sediment since it was constructed 150 years ago! 150 years... Did you know it was that old?

150 years, huh—

It's only a few feet deep in some parts now so they're going to dredge it up and make it deeper so it can sustain itself so they won't have to pump so much city water in. They'll coat it with some kind of liner to prevent water from leaking. Polymer? Yes, I think that's right. They raised something like seven million dollars!

Seven million, huh—

That was not what Ember wanted to be talking about.

She needed to know that Charlotte wasn't going to leave.

Honey, do you have to be in your head about everything?

Click click / click click

Hon-ey / Hon-ey

XVI. GARFIELD PARK CONSERVATORY

Iniquity can cage us or save us, depending on the light.

Charlotte took Ember to the Garfield Park Conservatory and seemed to have a wave of open curiosity for her for the first time since the beach day.

They poured in and out of each room slowly like lava.

There were so many green things to look at that Ember noticed nothing green in particular.

They stood in front of a plaque:

Sunlight takes thousands of years to be created, about eight minutes to reach Earth, and a fraction of a second to be captured and used by plants.

Sunlight is being captured. Notice light in the leaves above.

Look closely at any leaf. Sunlight is making things happen.

Charlotte's lips were a blanket of stone over her teeth.

Do you only reveal something if someone asks?

It took Ember a few beats of silence to realize that was probably true.

It happened so gradually she hadn't even noticed—

I think I used to do or say shocking things for attention when I was younger.

I know, I know…even younger than I am now.

They entered the desert room where everything had spikes and looked like it'd bite.

Ember admired the beige and tiny living stones and coral pink of the moonstone succulent. She pricked her finger on an Eve's Needle before reading *Please Do Not Touch!*

In some ways… Charlotte started.

…I think all you do is take. I've given you more about me than I've ever given anyone.

Ember took this less as a criticism and more like a compliment.

The two slowly made their way to the Aroid House with its little pond.

Condensation pasted the glass roof above.

Ember rubbed the bone at the base of her neck to get her blood flowing.

Pinched her suboccipitals and felt the muscle twitch.

She'd come up with her own verbiage for her head pain: her neck felt *crunchy*.

Her head often felt too heavy for her body. It pulled her forward but down.

Charlotte rubbed Ember's shoulder as if she'd forgotten they were in front of other people.

Ember didn't turn around. She didn't want to make a thing of it.

She became afraid any sudden movement might push Charlotte to realize what she was doing and stop.

Until she couldn't help it: she placed her hand over Charlotte's, stared ahead at the group of orange-banded catfish.

Together they counted sixteen royal-yellow decorative lily pads of blown glass patterned and spooled.

Ember told Charlotte how once, as a kid at the mall with Val, she saw a teenage couple on a bench outside the food court.

The boy was rubbing his girlfriend's neck, and Ember thought to herself:

I can't wait for that to happen to me.

The plaque said: *Air is moving. Look for blowing leaves.*

Air has substance. Feel the air touching you.

Water. Water moves from the roots to the stem through the branches to the leaves.

Water is all around you. Find water everywhere.

XVII. NEW YEAR

Edgy thoughts trespassed upon Ember's mind New Year's Day.

She considered she might be cursed—

Her mind bound to taint any chance for novelty or goodness. Root rot.

Ember couldn't seem to conceptualize the future beyond the next time she'd hear from Charlotte.

Something was off. Ember had always been able to feel slight shifts in Charlotte's cadence.

Time contracted and tightened, shucked Ember out of bed and down the hallway to the family room.

Family room, she thought, the name didn't quite fit.

Holidays meant Ember's dad was in town.

He watched the weatherman on TV from the loveseat and shuffled his feet: *-3° at Lake Michigan, feels like -25° with windchill.*

Spirits other than her own felt unusually high, curiously so.

Val was to prepare a simple brunch for the three of them, plus Ember's dad's parents.

Do you want me to make you a little something? You know before Grandma and Grandpa come?

Ember walked back to her room after agreeing to eggs over easy.

She overheard Val tell Ember's father: *Ember said* Thanks for the eggs, Mom. *But what she was really saying was she's proud of me.*

That was not what Ember was saying.

In fact, she found the times Val would try to get better even more devastating:

Val was alone in her own hope.

Ember wasn't so sure she even wanted Val to act as a mother at that point. She'd grown attached to her anguish.

Val swore at the stove from the kitchen.

Broke the yolk. Lit a cigarette.

At the dining room table with Ember's grandparents, her father transformed:

Told travel stories and talked through his laugh; the laugh eventually enveloped the words.

He held Val's veiny hand. Her many metal bracelets clinked.

Val never seemed to contribute a new thought to any conversation.

She only seemed to repeat what others said, only in a slightly different tone.

Ember winced at the thought of drawing attention to it.

Val's psyche was palpably fragile. Her eyes glazed and limp.

She stared at Ember from across the table—

An inverted scrutiny, as if she were staring at herself.

XVIII. CONTROLLED BURN

Ember entered an excruciating state of waiting.

Charlotte called an hour before to cancel their plan to meet on the east end of the pond while Jerry was at his weekly Monday basketball game.

She could feel something coming. She wanted to push Charlotte to do it just to prove it true.

Ember, have you ever heard of a controlled burn?

It's when they intentionally set fire to a forest during the cooler months to prevent fuel buildup so that there's not a more serious or hotter or destructive fire later on.

Why are you telling me this?

Listen, I don't want to hurt your feelings.

You couldn't hurt my feelings.

Why not?

Because I love you too much.

Wouldn't that mean I could hurt them more? You really should focus, you know, you've got your whole life ahead of you, college soon and...

...I envy you. Charlotte's voice was like a fingerprint.

Ember was stunned and very alive. *I don't want my whole life. I want you.*

Let's just let it rest for now, OK? You know we'll always be in contact.

Fuck you for leaving me. She slammed down the phone.

Slammed her bedroom door shut from the inside three big times until the wood around the knob split.

Opened her sock drawer and pulled out a translucent orange bottle half full of Stun she'd found the week before in an old purse in a pile of Val's purses in the basement.

Val must've taken too much she lost track—

She was terribly protective of her Stun. She'd drive with her purse next to her feet.

Ember chewed two on her way to the front door and sucked the taste of metal through her teeth.

Qu'est-ce qu'il y a?

Val, I don't fucking speak French!

Ember walked out into the moon-streaked night and leaked.

My whole life! She repeated it back to herself as if to make sense of it—

Felt a flush and a rush and a sway.

XIX. STUN HOLE

After that night Ember stayed in bed for three days and dipped in and out of time's seize.

She couldn't bear speaking to anyone or doing anything without Charlotte.

Ember had always lacked emotional skin. She felt agony at the slightest touch.

Stun became her iridescent armor.

On it she felt comfortable doing nothing. In fact, doing nothing was highly satisfying—

She felt whole and muffled.

A pill of sweat dripped down the small of her back.

She'd bite off another half to make the few Stun she had left last longer.

The more she took, the warmer she felt.

But the warmer she felt, the more she scratched her hot scalp like there was something she wanted underneath.

Scabbed her follicles. Felt pins and needles. A tick she couldn't shake until she had to shake her arm back to life from going numb—

Ember's arm above her head like that.

She concentrated on breathing, or else, she thought, it might not happen.

Her face went cell-pale.

Ember was not thinking about the way Charlotte looked at her on the beach while she was slinked in her seat pretending to read.

She was not thinking of Charlotte removing a splinter from the web between Ember's thumb and pointer finger.

She was not thinking about the intricate chalk white lines of the nerve plants on Charlotte's porch.

But it seemed as soon as her thoughts were emptied of Charlotte:

Charlotte came to mind.

PART THREE: TRIP

XX. NORTH SIDE

Lake Michigan felt like an ocean to Ember.

Ember was accepted into a college on the North Side of Chicago for a degree in book arts.

She'd heard once that if she couldn't figure out what to do with her life, she should go back to what brought her enjoyment when she was a kid.

Her first fall workshop was Book Design & Production. The assignment was to make a chapbook and leave the pages blank to take notes for the rest of the semester.

During this time the name Charlotte didn't feel safe in Ember's mind or mouth.

She tried to train herself to think of her as just *C*.

But even that was too painful, to think they were once close enough she could think of Charlotte as *her C*.

To really distance herself, Ember began to refer to Charlotte as if she were a title of a tarot card: The Magician, The Maverick, The Nightjar—

She thought she'd turn her failed love into an object—a page bouquet.

So Ember spent extra time in the lab to learn how to use the risograph printer. She selected the 50s-era typeface Klang, a brush script, to print *The Nocturne* on the cover.

She used Starch Rain Speckletone with tiny traces of thread like an old newspaper for the note pages and ebony black cardstock for an accent page.

She picked a soft-ribbed ochre paper with deckled edges for a cover. She enjoyed the precision of folding it with the grain into a dust jacket.

Ember used a single thread of silk-black linen to stitch through the folded pages at the spine.

Licked the cut thread before threading the needle. Poked the needle in her grooved fingertip.

Ember found the repetition meditative and calming, and tried to master it more each poke around.

It was in Book Design & Production she met Trip from Cleveland.

He was in his first year of college, on a scholarship for academics.

Trip was one year older than Ember. He'd spent a year after high school exploring California.

Ember felt he'd seen the edges of the earth.

The tips of Trip's shaggy hair were bleached frost-white.

He carried around a travel-sized bottle of hairspray. Tousle, spray.

Trip's shoulders were exceptionally pronounced—particularly his lateral deltoids, the tough tissues forming a cap.

His lips gravitated towards one corner when he spoke. He'd say, *Don't trip about it.*

The two spent most evenings together talking about things they thought as kids:

I thought the inside of hard boiled eggs was cheese.

I thought the gender of a child was determined by which parent was better in bed.

Ember would sleep on the floor of Trip's dorm room every Thursday before their early lab in the Book Arts department on Fridays.

He'd get in bed and pull the blanket up to his neck, close his eyes and say: *Want to see a trick?*

Trip would be perfectly asleep in under ten seconds.

Ember would watch his mouth soften like aging fruit.

XXI. DESTRUCTION & GROWTH

The lights in the gym gave Trip's triceps highlights.

On the street he was a sketch—in the gym he had breadth.

He practiced deadlifts in the floor-length mirror. Slowed down, exploded up.

Each session he noticed something different in the mirror. Some days it would be the well-developed triangle of his trapezius. Other days it would be vehemence, at eye level.

Racked the 25-lb plates carefully in their designated space.

Racked the 45-lb plates at the bench press.

His rep tempo: two-second positive contraction, four-second negative contraction, zero-second pause.

In the locker room, he pulled his headphones down around his neck, unzipped his gym bag.

The headphones fed him bodybuilding motivation:

Every day, have the inner strength to do something that moves you toward your goal: make it happen.

He poured two scoops of creatine and one scoop of electrolytes in his water bottle—flipped it upside-down, flipped it right-side-up, shook it purple.

All of Trip's muscles were built from little tiny tears.

In response they built stronger—more able to carry weights of the future.

Trip's quadriceps, in particular, protected him against strain, force, and the ever-present seismic shifts of the earth.

In high school, Trip lifted weights four days per week: Tuesday through Friday.

Tuesday: chest and shoulders. Wednesday: back and arms. Thursday: lower body. Friday: core and stability.

Every week he would progressively overload. He increased the reps or the resistance.

Or the time under tension. Or the rest between sets.

All the numbers were logged in a dedicated spiral notebook.

Eventually he began to train to failure, to shock his muscles and break through plateaus. Not failing was failing.

Even on rest days, he counted his carbs and protein. He had 1g of protein for every pound he weighed—mostly through pure whey protein powder and lean, air-chilled, no-water-added chicken breasts.

He prepared the chicken breasts in advance. Cooked until the juice ran clear. No butter, no salt.

Trip loved the routine of it. The repair of it, the recovery of it.

He slept eight hours every night, entered a constructed dreamworld. Bathed in Epsom salts and foam rolled.

He prioritized form over function. It was an aesthetic pursuit—a sculptural mastery.

By moving through the body's labyrinths, he accessed a world of tactile knowledge.

Ember never connected the look of Trip's sinews to the dedication it took.

And when the two met, the project of shaping his body's composition devolved gradually.

Stun first replaced core day—maybe he didn't really need it? (He'd had his core engaged during the other exercises the other three days, he thought.)

His thoughts were his body. Then they were not.

The naturally occurring dopamine and IGF-1 and endorphins and norepinephrine shifted synthetic.

He managed to convince himself of the value of periodic brush fires:

How they clear out undergrowth and release nutrients into the soil.

XXII. SAD PLANETS

Melancholy is mood and sorrow without any apparent cause.

Ember signed up for a philosophy class on humanity's place in the universe.

The instructor lectured on the root of the word *melancholy*:

Derived via Late Latin from Ancient Greek melancholía or 'condition of having black bile,' equivalent to melās 'black' and cholḗ 'bile, gall.'

Ember doodled little planets with moons and rings and frowns in her notebook.

Black bile was one of the four humors (along with blood, phlegm, and yellow bile).

Melancholy came to refer to the excess of the black bile—

The humors were associated first with climate and then seasons.

The matter outside of you matches the matter inside of you.

What was more valid, sorrow with or without apparent cause?

Ember boldly wondered.

Her thoughts darted in different directions like a startled murder of crows.

Val had given her a cause. Had Charlotte given her a cause? Would she have Charlotte's cause if she'd never had Val's?

Over the following days Ember became attracted to her own self destruction, too high on Stun to remember to eat. Not quite Stun chic—

More like black bile.

She'd nearly finished Val's lost bottle.

She had a dream about Charlotte. In the dream Ember was back working at the coffee shop by the pond.

Charlotte was walking into the coffee shop with a new hair color—soft black, shaking out an umbrella.

The dreaming continued while she was still awake, like stars in the sky during daylight.

She felt Charlotte through the mesh of her day, and looked out for her through her peripheral vision.

Back in Sad Planets—

Ember fidgeted with her ballpoint pen until it was almost broken. She unscrewed the barrel and the clip, then deconstructed the entire utensil. The ink cartridge, the spring, the thrust and plunge.

She felt the desire to push it to break. She could never live in the space between functional and garbage.

Melancholy was linked to seeking solitude.

The class watched a video on the projector screen of a deranged penguin in Antarctica running off into the wild, toward the mountains, away from the feeding grounds at the edge of the ice and away from the rest of his colony.

That was a level of removal that Ember couldn't even comprehend.

Ember had, in the past, wished for a different world.

Now she thought her cosmic insignificance might save her.

XXIII. DECODING

Ember and Trip entered a new era of attachment.

Even Trip's face looked different—his chin seemed to soften into his jawline.

She discovered multiple eye freckles, one the color of cinnamon floating from his iris into the white.

They referred to earlier memories as part of a time-period when they were less established: *Before we were us.*

It no longer struck her as odd that he used hairspray.

When Ember first moved into her dorm room, she felt sharply aware of her new furniture:

She wondered when her bed would start to feel less like a new bed and more like her own.

There was always an adjustment period where she existed on the outside of a new place, almost as if she were saying to herself: *If only I were here.*

But as soon as her bed and Trip felt familiar, she became superstitious.

She avoided the color red altogether. Before she made every trivial decision:

If I play this song or turn down this street, something bad will happen to Trip.

So much so that even thoughts of Charlotte felt buried—obscured.

It made her want to uncover them. If Charlotte lost meaning, what else was fleeting?

What was truly important? What would last?

She reposed in Stun's thready pulse.

As for what Stun meant to Trip—she could only speculate.

Second semester, Ember and Trip decided to share a two-bedroom apartment together in Lakeview.

They sat on their whisky-colored floor.

Scrolled through the homeware section of Craigslist:

DEPRESSION GLASS REAMERS AND DISPLAY CASE

*APPROXIMATELY ***50mg*** PIECES IN TOTAL*

ALL ORIGINAL, NO CRACKS, CHIPS OR REPAIRS

*ALL ***nutS*** AND BOLTS INCLUDED*

MORE INFO FOR INTERESTED PARTIES

Ember spoke: *Does that...*

...do you see what's in the asterisks?

Maybe they have to code it so that the post doesn't get taken down.

Do you think someone's really selling it?

I don't know. Let's message them and find out.

Thrill kicked inside of Ember like a pinball.

At the tip of sunset—

The two took the Blue Line to Six Corners to meet the Depression Glass Reamer dealer.

A mixture of metal and wind thrashed against the skyline.

Dozens of commuters walked up and down the platform faceless.

Is that him? A gulp sank in Ember's throat.

Then home to their apartment, dank and bare.

XXIV. PHOBIAS

What's for breakfast?

Well past noon—

Ember and Trip ate french fries at the lake and ashed the salt off as if each fry were a cigarette.

She saw the glow of her phone out of the corner of her eye:

She wasn't sure how long it'd been since she'd last heard from her father.

She took 30 Stun, her BSC was .93. They're pumping her stomach.

A bee traced salt in the wind and brushed Ember's fingertip.

Her father cleared his throat.

Ember shrilled as she felt the fuzz of a bee up the sleeve of her weathered T-shirt.

Are you OK?

Yes, sorry, there was just a bee on me. Are you at the hospital?

Val's weakness for Stun didn't necessarily erode their family dynamic; her weakness shaped it.

They'd grown used to her pattern: Val was always sick—either from not enough Stun or from too much.

Still the news hit crisp as glass.

Ember's father's voice spoke matter-of-fact about his wife's Stun-rich blood.

Ember went to the hospital more for herself. It was true: the hospital was one of the few places she felt safe.

She heard her dad's decade-old gym shoes squeaking against the vinyl floor as they walked. Pulled the curtain open to the hospital bay.

Val wore her oxygen tubes behind her ears like an accessory.

Val's throat was raw. She retched—

There were empty pockets where Ember's thoughts should be: tumbleweed through her brain cavities.

There was a period of reduced blood flow, so she might have some memory loss.

Loss of motor skills...balance, coordination.

Ember felt a specific sensation she only experienced while witnessing physical vulnerability. She felt the same shiver seeing Val's mom's dark-spotted hands shake with age.

Ember's emotions often manifested with physical intensity—

She had all types of flushes: flowing over her nose when she felt observed, under her collarbones when she felt uncomfortable telling the truth, and a full-face flush trying to stand her ground.

Trip would always welcome them: *Hello Flush 1, Flush 2, Flush 3.*

Back with him at sunfall—

I heard about this thing in my Psych class, catching 'fleas.'

Like 'lie down with the dogs you're bound to catch fleas?'

Yes, like that, when children who grow up with a narcissist start to emulate their behaviors...

...maybe you're catching Val's Stun fleas.

Was Ember taking Stun because it was addictive, or was Ember taking Stun because she was like Val?

Was there a difference? She needed to derail.

Suddenly it seemed trivial to fear bees.

XXV. CLOUDS

Trip had a special affinity for the weather.

Do you see the cloud formation? That's really interesting.

The wind is usually blowing this way...

He moved his hands west to east like a meteorologist on CNN swiping around the country.

...because of the jet stream. But today we're getting easterly winds...

He swiped east to west in a swirl.

...so it's colder than usual. Don't you guys have a saying here in Chicago? 'If you don't like the weather...'

They said in unison, their tone brash: *Wait ten minutes.* A cliché they thought was fresh.

Ember and Trip walked to a greenhouse in Edgewater in search of specific plants for their apartment.

Trip had learned everything about cockroach deterrents. Their least-favorite scent was eucalyptus.

But mint would work in a pinch.

By the time they arrived, Trip could see faint sundogs over the lake.

Inside the nursery dome—

An older woman sat on a lawn chair with neon ripstop fabric.

She faced the entrance, but her eyes seemed out of focus. Trip thought cataracts: *Clouds as eyes.*

The clouds rolled in the back of her head and swallowed everything—not like a moon or an eclipse, but like a nightmare.

Gasped herself awake. Ember jumped like a flea, matched her gasp.

The woman's mouth reminded Ember of Val's. It wasn't so much the actual lips or teeth as it was a severe expression of Val's mannerisms.

The woman noticed Ember and Trip. Wiped spit from her cracked lip.

Mumbled: *Are you folks...looking for something?*

Her misted eyes framed by the strings of her hair.

Yes, ma'am. Do you have eucalyptus or mint plants?

And maybe something small and low-maintenance...

Trip elbowed Ember *...you know, to liven the place up?*

What's your house number?

3931.

Street?

Ashland.

Is your apartment facing the street or the alley?

Alley.

You can have any of these that are on the left because they're low-light succulents.

The eucalyptus and...mint are on the back wall.

Ember was between a snake plant and an ox-tongue plant.

She always had a fondness for bonsai trees, but doubted her ability to grow or take care of one.

Trip collected the eucalyptus determinedly. Hugged the pot, inspected the succulent.

His attention poured from shelf to shelf.

What do you think of this one?

Ember had never felt more like she was part of a team.

I just want to make sure you like it too.

I do like it.

Ok, then this is the one.

They brought the eucalyptus plant, Ember's snake plant, and Trip's baby bonsai tree up to the woman, who opened her metal moneybox with a key clipped to her waist.

Next to the moneybox was crumpled tinfoil with burnt blue resin and a Zippo lighter.

Later, sitting on the fire escape facing the back alley—

The two smoked cigarettes and the city coughed.

You know that woman at the greenhouse today? Ember asked.

She saw something in Trip's throat: an omission, a rapid swallowing of air.

A pigeon landed next to them—on their bags of trash, sticky with pop.

Let's go inside, Trip said.

He grabbed the metal banister and swung upward like a wrecking ball.

XXVI. OBSESSIONS

Ember's painting instructor was terrifically embodied.

In this class we will be painting our obsessions.

I want you to get ahold of the thing that has a hold on you.

What is the still point in your turning world?

I want you to introduce yourself to its landscape.

Obsessions come from the body.

Just thinking about your obsession releases oxytocin.

It stimulates the production of nitric oxide...

...which expands the tissues in the heart.

The way we feel in our body can change our thoughts.

What makes you simmer? What makes you explode? What makes you, you?

Is it a phenomenon in the sky, a marathon run, a habit or a crutch?

Forget what you want to paint for someone else.

What do you need *to paint?*

Ember always wanted to change her thoughts but couldn't figure out how.

She dedicated a corner of their living room to her stretched canvas and monochrome-powdered paint.

Outside the clouds pinned the sun.

Stun released ice-cream scoops of dopamine. Too much Stun caused *neuron death.*

You'd lose the ability to feel good. But equally you couldn't feel as bad.

She made hundreds of micro-decisions each time she bit into one—chewing the Stun so her stomach wouldn't take the time to break it down. Its metallic grit in her teeth.

Something her painting instructor said must have made her more aware of a gut instinct:

Stun may not be quite what her body needed.

What was it she needed then? In the mirror she searched for an answer.

Ember's head looked too big for her body.

The skin around her mouth was scaling: patchy and parched.

Her twenty-year-old face surprised her.

Trip materialized in the bathroom doorway: *I heard something in class about how if you ask someone how old they are in their head...*

...they immediately grasp what you mean.

I feel about eight.

Eight years old? Trip seemed rather shocked but Ember stuck by it.

She began to paint circles pale-gray—reflections of wispy halos around a half-moon:

A picture of a pond in the night.

XXVII. OVERLAP

Ember woke up inside the image of Val in the Emergency Room.

Val was resilient, Ember had to admit: seemingly indestructible.

She always imagined her mother in terms of temperature: too warm, bursting, a notch before ignition.

She needed to move. Or more accurately, she needed to trade bad feelings. She'd be willing to feel something equally as bad, as long as it was different.

Stepped into Trip's bedroom to wake him—

Ember saw he'd written on a small dry-erase board on the back of his door:

DO PUSH-UPS

IT'S OK

Spoke: *Do you want to come with me to the South Side for the day?*

There's a pond with a lot of ducks.

She knew that'd get him. Trip plain loved ducks.

He had a bag of a hundred little rubber ducks from the 99¢ store and he'd gift them out on special occasions.

He used the rubber ducks as a way to measure someone's significance in his life.

Would he give them a duck, or was he hesitant?

Once this bag is out, that's it.

Ember's windowsill in her bedroom had a team of three.

Trip requested they stop at the corner store to pick up oats to feed the ducks.

He carried the entire 10-pound sack with him on the L.

Balanced the sack on the ground between his feet, gripped a subway pole.

Each time the doors opened he stepped off with the sack and stood to the side to make way for an exit.

Commuters shimmied. A curl of hair slipped out of his Guardians cap. He stepped back on the train.

Then came the Metra. They sat, and Trip put his feet on the bag.

When Ember and Trip reached Echo Pond, the North Lawn was fenced off.

A canvas map and a timeline on the east end detailed the restoration.

By summer they'd start the dredging operation, making it three feet deeper to better sustain itself.

Ember shook her head back and forth in micromovements: the whole undertaking impressed her.

Trip had a band of mallards eating oats from his hand.

Ember imagined she might see Charlotte in the park.

A daydream of sorts: one that made her ribs swell.

She needed Charlotte to see her with Trip. Yes—Charlotte would see a version of her that was light.

No—she needed Charlotte to know she was unconditionally devoted to her.

She never really did consider if the two were a couple, what would people think of them?

Maybe, she figured, she knew she would never have to.

A blue heron basked on a log. A flutter of butterflies shook off the dust.

XXVIII. EVENT HORIZON

The sky cracked open and it was winter.

On the way out of his astrophysics lecture, Trip heard his classmate say on the phone:

Bring money, we're Stunning!

He couldn't stand the recreational reference. For Trip, there was nothing fun about Stun.

Maybe at the start, for a fevered pocket of time.

What happened in California was still stitched behind his eyes:

He'd never tell Ember what happened to him there.

He'd only imagine scraping into his skin to pull it out.

When he arrived in Chicago, the invisible black hole lingered behind him.

A grid illusion: flickers of tiny black dots.

Trip skirted the event horizon without crossing it. Flickers of white light—aimed outward, with velocity.

He fused with Ember. The clock locked.

Trip red-shifted into infinity. Became faint, stretched out.

Trip arrived in his bedroom. His suitcase from a summer visit to Cleveland lay by his bed, still packed.

He opened his dresser drawer. Inside was an empty half-pint of ice cream.

He grabbed the nearest clothing item: yesterday's jeans. Chocolate stain? He convinced himself denim was self-cleaning.

In the bathroom he pulled all of the tissue out of the tissue box.

Removed some tinfoil, a gummed blue. Stuffed back the tissue, fluffed the puffing piece.

He turned the coffee machine on. The coffee machine turned off. He turned the coffee machine on again.

He lit a flame under the tinfoil. Went back to the coffee machine. Pressed the start button but forgot the coffee.

Ember's father convinced her to visit Val in the psychiatric ward for Family Day.

Trip needed to remember to call her at 1:00 pm.

He told Ember he'd call. He'd wanted to call. She'd needed him to call.

It was important that he called. But 1:00 pm became 1:07 pm, and by then, it was no longer 1:00 pm.

So the task to call Ember at 1:00 pm must have been complete, he thought, because otherwise it would not be 1:07 pm. Stun heated, whipped metallic blue smoke. Trip drank a coffee mug full of hot water.

He sat down on the couch. He crossed his legs. He uncrossed his legs. He crossed his legs again.

He bit the skin between his thumb and his pointer finger. Rubbed the chocolate stain further into the stitch.

Trip stood up and in front of the full-length mirror. Turned his head, his shoulders—inspected his lats.

The strength was still there, underneath. He just needed the right light.

His body seethed back. He needed to detach. He needed to step away to remain intact.

XXIX. THE DYNAMIC OCEAN

The lake was a frozen map and there was a lag in every clock.

Ember waited on the corner of Belmont and Clark for the 22 down to campus.

She sucked in three last puffs of a cigarette—

Exhaled with a squeak and a crackle.

The CTA driver yelled to her: *Get on the damn bus.*

Heat slithered out the folding doors.

Ember flicked the filter right at the front wheel. Stepped on with the sound of January slush.

Her bus pass wouldn't take: *OUT OF FUNDS.*

The driver shook his head, gestured his head towards the back: *Just get on the damn bus!*

Ember was determined to show up for her oceanography class:

She wasn't going to be a dropout like Val.

No—there was a lot to say for someone who could follow through.

In the Arts & Letters building on campus—

Ember walked into The Dynamic Ocean lecture a little too dosed.

The more Stun that Ember took, the more she needed. It seemed she couldn't quite—

—get comfortable.

She removed her hoodie and draped it on the back of her chair.

She removed her hoodie from the back of the chair and wriggled back inside of it.

Her hot flash flipped inside out. She had the goosebumps of a fever.

Yes—her body was a harsh shade of red.

She felt she might float out of her chair if she didn't hold on—gripped the seat tight with her wiry thighs.

Ember couldn't seem to hem down a single soupy thought.

On a crunchy walk home in the snow—

She called Trip and got a dial tone. Rehearsed a voicemail for him she'd never leave.

Trip hadn't been home or answered his phone in three days.

In the gloom of twilight—

He messaged Ember from an unknown number:

Hey, it's me. I met a girl and have been hanging out with her a lot. Can you water my bonsai? Thx.

Well just fuck off then.

Why does it have to be all or nothing?

Ember thought hard about Trip's response. Why *did* it have to be all or nothing?

She couldn't come up with an answer.

In their bathroom of grit—

Ember took both sets of fingernails and ran them down her opposing arms.

But she needed more feeling. She took an X-Acto knife from her book arts bag and slit short and deep vertically down her left forearm.

Blood popped up like a garnet duck egg.

Ember managed to retain one thing in The Dynamic Ocean:

There is a difference between an underwater explosion and an underwater implosion.

In an implosion, the force acts violently *inward.*

She removed all of the tissue out of the tissue box and taped the tissue over her ruptured arm.

The last of it mudded with dark blue.

XXX. STUN BAKE

Do you ever put a hot pan under running water?

I heard that's primarily a male impulse—

Trip asked, if only to make conversation.

The sink smoked and hissed.

Did you hear that from your new girl?

Trip had stopped by their apartment for the first time all week to bake a batch of Stun brownies for a date with Iris.

The process was actually really simple:

Suck on the Stun until the blue coating flakes off.

Crush it down to a very fine dust, spread it evenly across a piece of tinfoil.

Put a flame underneath the tinfoil. Melt it down to a burnt blue resin.

Mix the resin in with melted butter. Add the butter to melted chocolate.

I've been adding extra vanilla.

Oh, and coconut sugar to help cover up the metallic taste.

Where'd you get the Stun from?

Some new guy, for a lot cheaper.

Ember hummed.

She'd developed an incessant ringing in her ears—couldn't remember when it started.

Do you have something against Iris, or what?

She concentrated on his eye freckle—felt skinned in her seat.

Do you want me to sit around and be depressed too?

No. But if you were depressed...

...I'd want you to be depressed about me.

Ember realized how juvenile it sounded the second it dumped out of her mouth.

The air between them simmered.

Trip exited so quickly he spun.

This was a multiple Stun affliction.

Ember was running out. She messaged the Glass Reamers Dealer.

You need nutS? I have some other shit too if u want.

Like what?

It's like nutS but pure.

Comes in a tar. U have to smoke it.

Just start slow. U will like it.

Nine minutes passed before Ember responded.

Mostly she stared out the window—her judgment minced.

Thanks, but I'll just take 10 nutS.

I'll meet you at the corner at 4.

Ok.

Don't text me 'ok'

Ember typed *Ok* and then deleted it.

She kneaded through the next hour: halved her last Stun and parachuted it.

By the face of dusk—

Ember stewed in her sweat-drenched bed.

Ate Cheerios straight from the box, mouthed to no one: *Out of milk.*

She nodded off until her fist unclenched and she fell asleep until morning:

Crushed Os all over the sheets.

XXXI. STUN MATH

Ember started looking for trouble so it didn't catch her by surprise.

She ran out of money from the cafe and birthdays, and asked Glass Reamers Dealer to spot her.

Borrowed $485 worth of Stun in the first week. $500 was his debt limit for all customers—

No exceptions, no quarter orders.

Every Tuesday she'd owe him 20% for the *juice* until she chipped away at the *principal.*

Ember needed a prescription. Plan: Sell 1/3 to Glass Reamers to cover two weeks of juice.

The rest, personal stash. It'd force her to stick to the prescribed amount while she got some money together.

Yes, she told herself, *then I'll be normal.*

It would cost $15 to see the doctor—the copay for the FDA's PPO plan she was under until 26. With insurance, the Stun prescription itself would cost $2.50.

In the Great Hall of Union Station a man sat slumped over on a bench with a syringe in his hand.

The back of his rib cage expanded and collapsed in short desperate bursts.

Ember waited four and a half minutes off to the side. Her train left in twelve minutes. She had at least a five-minute walk through the station.

The man's face was covered between his knees; he was folded in half.

But she could see his hands had gone pale—were they blue? She listened closely for any little gasp.

Decided to dial 9-1-1 as she kept walking to the platform headed Southwest to New Lawn.

A burst of flashing color floated in her field of vision.

Blinding red: the blood from Val biting her tongue the night she was eight. Shaking.

Outside the sun was surely rising, fighting against the wind.

On the top level of the double-decker train, Ember watched an old man in a tweed flat cap look out the window in a state of content.

No book, no music. What was going on there?

Her nerves were stretched out like the strings of a guitar.

Upon arrival, she cut through the wood chips of a playground to the immediate care center.

She made espresso-sized circles with her ankles in the waiting room.

Stun dominated a plastic carousel of medicinal brochures.

Are you impulsive? Disorganized? Problems following through and completing tasks? Hot temper?

Extended release of Stun in the bloodstream could be for you.

In exponentially smaller type, a warning: *Sudden Death and Pre-existing Structural Cardiac Abnormalities or Other Serious Heart Problems.*

Regular use or abuse can make changes in the brain and change how you regulate emotions.

Stun raises blood pressure, body temperature, and heart rate.

Stun can keep users awake and stimulated while suppressing appetites.

Tell your doctor if you start to experience pains in your heart muscles, lungs, vascular system, or other internal organs.

Amber? A nurse called her in without looking up from her clipboard.

She checked Ember's pulse; Ember could feel the nurse's warm breath on her wrist.

Height: 5'3". Weight: 99 lbs. Went faint from the blood pressure monitor: 140/90 mmHg.

The nurse reported the vital sign results rather matter-of-factly—

Ember couldn't tell if she was void of worry, or disguising her worry for Ember's sake.

What brings you in today?

Through the window: the sharp sound of a jackhammer tore up the main road in New Lawn.

I've been having trouble focusing in classes and was hoping to talk to the doctor about a solution.

I don't really want any medicine...

...but if it were medically necessary: reverse reverse reverse psychology.

The doctor walked in; he was so tall it was like an optical illusion.

He didn't exactly look like Ember's father, but he had his affect.

A notable lack of flexibility in his neck: his whole body moved to turn his head.

The doctor slid over to her on a stool with wheels.

Where do you go to school?

Up north.

Have you heard of Stun?

I think so—scrunch of the mouth.

It's very effective for the type of thing you're experiencing.

Do you have a local pharmacy?

Walgreens on 87th—it's by my parents.

Plan: Go home and find her father's checkbook.

Call if you have any problems.

Write a check to herself and cash it while they fill the script.

Her life had demarcated there in Walgreens:

Now she was as accomplished a liar as Val.

She remembered dialing 9-1-1 for the collapsed man at the station. Was that the same day?

Maybe he'd been trying to die. Maybe she'd messed that up, too.

XXXII. LOVE, HATRED, & RESENTMENT

Essence is the basic, real, and invariable nature of a thing.

Ember woke up in the bad apartment.

Her phone said 11:04 am.

It didn't *feel* like morning, she thought. Ember's internal clock was a lawless land.

Still no messages from Trip: the day disintegrated.

Ember had a trick to force herself out of bed:

She'd tell herself: *I have to stay in bed for the rest of my life. I have to stay in bed for the rest of my life. I have to stay in bed for the rest—*

She rolled over and her back cracked like bubble wrap.

The whole space felt dormant:

The furniture was asleep, the pots and pans were asleep, the plants were dead.

Ember only waited three minutes after getting up to snort a Stun.

Flames raced up under her right eye—morphed into a tear.

She sneezed blood all over the sink. The blood wouldn't clot; she laid her head back in bed.

Ember's mind was an eggshell—her wit brittle.

She always imagined she loved Trip in the purest form:

Was it still love if she wanted him to be happy *only* if it were with her?

She thought hard about this notion; all of her thoughts felt like lies.

A sustained clench of the jaw forced her temples to swell.

The drum of her blood vessels—an elusive itch.

Decided to send Trip a message: *Can we talk now?*

Her phone glowed and her rib quivered.

She imagined the same feeling was once evoked when people saw handwritten envelopes in their mailbox.

People don't write letters enough anymore, she declared to herself. Maybe she'd make Trip a chapbook.

I'm so sorry about Trip. What happened?

The message wasn't from Trip; it was from someone in their class.

Thanks, Ember typed back. *It's just some bullshit.*

Ember felt trapped and observed like a spider in a jar.

Days passed that week with listlessness; Friday vanished into night.

She walked down the hallway to Trip's bedroom: the clicking of plywood.

Inside, emptiness. The carpet was a different color where the furniture had been—clean. Plus one spot in the shape of a suitcase.

Ember turned over the door to the dry erase board:

IT'S OK

Ember was still and numb as a cliff's edge.

In essence, she knew, Trip was not coming back.

Not for light. Not for material. Not for any amount of matter.

She pulled her deeply heavy body to bed. She supposed she would not be awake for much longer.

In the moments leading to total oblivion she tried to recall every part of Trip's bedroom:

His bonsai tree and his rubber ducks and his goddamn hair spray.

PART FOUR: ONE ELEVEN POND

XXXIII. ONE ELEVEN POND

Time passed. Strawberry season became tomato season.

A chef purchased the warming shelter across from Echo Pond and renovated the space into a farm-to-table fine dining restaurant.

Stacks of plates slumbered under a heat lamp in the window of the open kitchen.

Some slates. Aqua-blue splattered in navy, coral print and rimmed in white. Ceramic carafes.

The silverware had little etches: proof they were crafted by the simple, honest, and hardworking.

Line cooks in paisley bandanas and beet-stained aprons rushed around the corners yelling *Knife!*

Ember watched a waiter serve a table on the patio. The *tiniest* plate, she thought:

It seemed there were a hundred words for one fine bite of food.

The menu had items Ember had never heard of: tomato gazpacho, fennel lemonade, peach tepache.

Citrus-cured fish, buttermilk granita, dehydrated watermelon rind.

Above the bar, a quote painted on the wall in vintage script:

Birds here make song, each bird has his,

Across the girdling city's hum.

Ember approached a wooden podium.

Shifted her weight; feigned eye contact by looking at the host's mouth.

I used to work here when it was a café…I'm home from college and was wondering if you might need any help?

We are looking for a backwaiter. Can you come in for a stage?

A stage?

Yes, it's like a paid trial shift.

Oh, right, of course.

How about tomorrow at 5:00 pm?

Ember tried to come up with a reason to delay. Couldn't find one—searched for *Yes.*

Wear black pants, black button-up shirt, and black non-slip shoes. We'll give you the tie and apron.

What was your name, Amber did you say?

It's Ember.

You can take home one of these menus if you like.

Description of the first course: *A bed of macerated raspberries and coconut poppyseed custard.*

Main course: *Braised ox cheek with kimchi caramel sauce and potato curry pie.*

On her way out she watched a man in a white chef's jacket watering plants on a rooftop garden.

The building was on a grassy hill; the path would take you right up.

He sprayed the hose onto the side landscaping. It crashed against the windows and onto bushes of squash and watermelon and berries.

A beekeeper was on the other end of the roof tending to a colony of honeybees.

The dredging operation for the pond had begun.

Waterless, a blue heron sat on a mound of dirt looking at the cranes with a cocked beak.

Ember saw a woman greet a new table on the patio as she was leaving:

It was Charlotte with a black napkin in her apron—

A winged wine key in her back pocket reflecting like a blade.

XXXIV. DESIRE

The sight of Charlotte was retina-burn from an eclipse.

What are you doing here?

Jerry and I split this year, so I had to find a place of my own.

I used to waitress in Pittsburgh so...

...here I am.

I hear you'll be my assistant tonight.

Ember sensed Charlotte trying not to smile.

The silence stretched out like bubblegum.

Max will show you around while we get ready for service.

She gestured towards the prep kitchen where a man in a hairnet rolled dough intently.

He looked up. *So, I know you know the space because you used to work here, but it's changed a lot.*

Charlotte will tell you mostly what to do throughout the night...

...but here is where we store the bread rolls that every table gets.

If they are gluten-free you give them this. He pointed to white rolls.

If they are vegetarian you give them this. He pointed to wheat rolls marked with a cross.

Otherwise they are durum wheat rolls with country ham and cultured butter.

We use these tongs to serve them.

When your front waiter greets the table, look out for the signs on what kind of water to bring.

So if Charlotte taps her hand—he tapped the top of his right hand with his left—*then you bring tap water.*

Wiggled his fingers for sparkling water. Hand out with palm facing the floor for flat.

Crumb the table in between courses with this thing: Max showed Ember a curved aluminum tool with a pocket clip.

Don't stack the plates at the table, clear from the right.

Pick up big plates first, then small, then silverware. It's just easier that way.

Don't throw your plates in the dish pit too hard, it splashes Jasper and it's not very nice.

She looked for Charlotte through the swinging door of the kitchen.

That's about it. The barista and food runners will do everything else.

I'll go over the table numbers while we mop.

If you pick it up, they'll promote you to front waiter pretty quick and you can make a lot more money.

Are you 21?

Not quite.

Oh OK, then I guess you'll stick to backwaiting. Best thing about it is you don't have to talk to anybody.

How had this building shifted from *her* space to *Charlotte's* space? It wasn't fair.

Do you want some water? We have to drink out of these plastic deli containers.

If glass breaks near the service well we have to burn all the ice.

There's a soda gun behind the bar if you want Coke or something.

In the pre-shift meeting, the chef from the roof introduced a new dessert with sweetcorn.

Charlotte said: *Chef, I know this is the Midwest—*

But they're already suspicious about the pea cremeux.

Ember's laugh hit like a red sprite.

Condensation from the air vents dripped onto the back of her neck.

She felt an intense desire to be alone with Charlotte.

She worried if the two waited too long, there'd be a jump cut to their new dynamic:

Their relationship a compression artifact.

XXXV. DARK SIDE

Saturday nights felt like a theater performance at One Eleven Pond.

The Feels Like temperature was 103 degrees with humidity—

Forced a power outage across the entire park district and broke the fourth wall.

Jasper came out of the dish pit to find a dining room filled with oven smoke.

Chef said *Keep moving!* until Ember's braid unraveled.

Charlotte told Ember to pop her head around to the sauté station to tell them: *Fire table 26*.

The sauté station? Ember inspected all of the line cooks.

One was prepping amuse-bouche and cheese boards with sticky fig relish and fresh raw honeycomb from the roof bees. Another had bundles of pasta in nests and pads of butter.

The cook at the far left end with scale-like burns up his arm sliced a duck breast into lanières.

Charlotte asked me to tell you fire table 26.

Fuck Charlotte. Grease from his pan frothed and crackled.

Nothing to do but shut early. All of the guests from the 7:00 seating left before their main course.

The team moved to the roof for a meeting; the maître d' opened a bottle of sparkling wine without making a pop.

Charlotte whispered in Ember's ear: *Since we didn't make any money tonight...*

...do you want to go make some?

What'd you say?

Do you want to go make some money?

She didn't hear Charlotte again. The first time was an outline, the second time nearly filled it in.

I've noticed you sneaking off. Grinding your teeth. We can get you some Stun. Jasper's got some.

Ember imagined she'd always be able to sense the existence of Stun.

She was perversely impressed she didn't realize about Jasper: Stun really was omnipresent.

Charlotte and Ember headed east on Echo Path.

Every step of the way Ember had the feeling she was missing something—couldn't place if it was a possession or thought or emotion.

A man with a straight-brimmed Cubs hat flashed the headlights of his Jeep, nodded upwards.

So, how do you know Charlotte? Hat-man asked Ember with no inflection.

We work together.

Right, OK. We've got young blood in the car, Ricky. He yelled out the door to his friend on the phone.

Do you want some of this?

It was the bright blue tar she saw when she was with Trip at the greenhouse.

The friend got in the car and shut the door with the sharp edge of a drill.

Ember thought hard about the word *panic.*

Too hard—thought she might choke on the word running deep circles through the backseat.

No, thanks. I really only take the pills.

It's basically the same thing. Plus, we have this here if anything happens to you. It's an antidote: we'll just spray it up your nose and it'll block the Stun receptors in your brain.

This moment felt like a hingepoint: a lateral branch of a tree.

Don't do anything you don't want to do, honey. Charlotte rubbed both of her shoulders, lit a menthol.

Shall we drive a bit?

Ember made a conscious choice to loosen up.

I'll say Yes *to everything else tonight*, she thought. *Just not that.*

Charlotte put her lips hard and smooth as marble to Ember's—

Rolled her tongue on the back of Ember's shaking teeth.

She unbuttoned Ember's pants and laid her down on the hot dark leather.

Ember thought about Trip. She thought about clouds and school and the moon.

All three took turns sticking their fingers inside of her. She thought: as long as the men are touching her and not Charlotte.

She saw the cruel flash of a camera and a lick of Hatman's lips.

The car was parked; they'd made it to the industrial part of the South Side.

Ember's world went a new shade of black—her legs shook her back to real time.

She pulled her pants above her waist and they drove back to where they started.

The August moon reflected on the sidewalk. If she were anybody else, she thought, it'd be a beautiful night.

At the edge of the path—

Charlotte told Ember *I'll be right out.* Charlotte's eyelids were both sunken-in and swollen like dough.

Ember went towards a temporary wooden bridge that stretched over the dredged-up pond from east to west.

She walked across and stood above the bed of mud. At 1:00 am the truth was fleeting in the dark.

What was Charlotte doing?

She ambled back to the Jeep with eerie detachment.

The back door was open. Charlotte's body was loose at 90 degrees and Hat-man was pushing inside her from behind.

Ember's chest knitted. *Get the hell off her!*

Charlotte wailed like a stuck piano key: told Ember to stay out of it and *Go home.*

A light came on from a mid-rise apartment complex overlooking the park—went out.

She couldn't get lost: either she'd hit the highway or the interstate.

Ember walked the streets without a scrap of fear or heart.

XXXVI. AFTERWARDS

The air was tinted obsidian and checkered with dread.

The earth had folded; Ember felt right up against its carbon walls.

Cottonwood fell from the trees like ash.

She imagined the night; the night turned into a memory.

Ember blamed Charlotte.

She blamed Val and Trip and the men in the car and all cars and everyone and the pond.

She aged like a spirit in a copper still.

She was flooded with a clear honest desire to leave the city for good.

When does the way you behave become part of your character?

Ember daringly wandered.

XXXVII. CHERRY

Ember recognized the strange man in her kitchen from a photograph.

Per her father's request she had emerged from her bedroom—one of the first times that week.

Ember!

Meet Jerry. The two shook hands like salesmen.

He works with me at the FDA in the artificial flavors sector but is thinking of joining the dark side with CDER.

Ha ha ha.

Try a sip of this cocktail he made.

Jerry asked Ember with a sinister twinkle: *What does it taste like to you?*

She took a sip from her father's glass coupe. *Cherry?*

Ahh.

To some people benzaldehyde tastes like cherry and to others it tastes like almond.

I have a theory about who tastes what.

Ember forced a cough.

Jerry looked at her with total annihilation.

Shall we all go out on the deck?

Life trickled into the old white oaks. One took a breath, shed an acorn.

A woman with a sand-blonde bob cradled an infant in the shade. They looked exactly right, Ember noted: a contained brilliance.

Val pinched the lit end of a half-cigarette out into a dry patch in the grass—put it back in the pack.

Jerry placed a broad hand over the woman's shoulder. *This is my wife, Eve, and our daughter, Belle.*

Ember held out her pointer finger for the baby to squeeze.

Did everyone feel as acutely as she did?

Ember sensed an onion-skin film between Val and the group.

Tuned into the noise of the high-voltage cables from the power lines.

Val asked to hold Belle—

She took deep red leaps over to the above-ground pool. Held her by the underarms over the water and let her little feet splash.

The pool was four feet deep. A cardinal in the backyard let out a short metallic chip.

Ember's father snaked off the deck and darted over to Val, eyes ablaze.

He reached over the pool and scooped Belle to his chest. Muttered something soft and severe as a cut of flesh.

Val stepped back, dipped her chin. *It was nice to meet you but...*

...I'd better go back inside. Ember followed behind, and walked straight through the house and out the front door. Above, the sky expanded its faceless clouds.

XXXVIII. EMBER WRITES A LETTER TO TRIP

You were in my dream last night.

We decided to walk home along the Missouri River (which ran, in this case, from St. Louis to Chicago) and kept almost falling in.

I've been designing maps and going on extraordinarily long walks.

Ended up at a gallery today. I saw an installation: A series of notes that were all addressed to a 'you.'

They were as if the artist had lost contact with an old lover and hoped if they made this art installation, it'd end up in a gallery, and the old lover would then possibly maybe visit the gallery, wander into the exhibition, and read the letters.

I just wish we could have been sustainable and net-positive.

I know, I know—Those are boring terms for something so fierce.

Maybe sustainable, net-positive, and on fire.

Every shop I went into today, I looked for things you'd like.

I looked for buildings you'd like, especially abandoned ones.

I looked carefully through the windows, and didn't once catch my own reflection.

A lot has happened since we last spoke: Leaves fell off the trees. The clock ticked quickly and loudly. I felt eight years old again, I felt twelve, I turned twenty-two the day the supermoon was at 100%.

Lost my way and took the train home after it all.

Learned from the guy across from me that when trains were invented, people were worried humans wouldn't be able to handle the speed—that they would be so fast, rides would liquify our insides, and even horses and cows would drop down dead if they were anywhere near a train passing.

I don't think I'll ever forget this one thing you said to me.

It's fun to play little games with my brain like that!

Every time the thought pops up, I have to practice remembering it, and bringing it forth—and then I think, 'Is this going to be one of those things I remember and think about after years and years?'

Can we force that?

XXXIX. THE NOCTURNE (A CHAPBOOK)

I held a hot pot of glass
the color of your eyes.
I looked at the color of your eyes,
you looked around the night,
we looked inside.
The night spilled fire,
our skin expanded,
we shaped together into a sphere.
I named the color of your eyes moon-blue,
you spilled inside of me.
You set in a small amount of air,
we became a pattern, we spooled.
A thin layer of glass cooled,
I spilled inside of you,
we filled up the chamber.
Last week we were uniformed,
a complete outfit.
Next week you are a novel set of notes.
A powdered color, a mold.
For me, for your hand on my face.
Today I am already somebody different.

XL. A BEAUTIFUL DAY IN CHICAGO THAT NEVER HAPPENED (A CHAPBOOK)

A sky scratched with white clouds. An invisible wind on an otherwise clear Midwestern morning.

•

Two simultaneous near-death experiences happen on opposite sides of town, but no one is hurt.

One nearly occurs on a bicycle. The cyclist is rattled—decides to buy a helmet, decides she's only got the one head, eats a bowl of shredded wheat and enjoys it in a new way.

The other which nearly happens to a driver. She shifts her arm from acting as a second seatbelt for her daughter in the passenger seat to tapping her daughter's knee in relief.

•

A ten-year-old boy watches his mother in the kitchen while she cuts up a watermelon. He practices using chopsticks by picking out all the seeds.

He helps his mother with the dishes. Washes a water glass with hot water, turns the tap and fills it up with cold water to drink. It cracks in his hand into two perfect pieces—no broken skin, no blood shed.

A lilac scented wood-wick candle burns in the connecting living room.

•

It is a woman's first day of retirement after working for the Department of the Treasury for thirty-five years. She scans the hair dye aisle in Walgreens for a 'fun' color: dark tulip, sky blue, clementine. Settles on hot pink.

Her husband comes home after eighteen holes of golf.

He gasps. She winces. He approaches, runs his fingers through the neon streak.

I love it, *he tells her, and he genuinely means it.*

They take a walk near the lake—spot a dinghy with a bit of grass sprouting through the crack of the seat.

They seem to have the afternoon all figured out.

•

A wristwatch tells the wrong time. A woman thinks she's arrived too early, breathes sharply before entering a cottage blend brick restaurant.

But the minute tick was off—she's right on time. Her first date is waiting by the host podium with two menus.

A mediocre song plays on the radio in the background but sounds much better than they both remember.

It's an exciting realization for the two. They suspect probably because it's familiar, and selected beyond their control.

•

I realize: It takes a lot for me to bury a feeling. This can actually be a very good thing.

A few thoughts later: how plenty happens if you think about minutiae.

I bend over to pick up a penny face-up on the sidewalk, but then decide to leave it for the next person.

The planet is not so sad.

•

And you. I forgot to mention you.

My cell phone buzzes right as I finish an insurmountable task I'd been putting off.

I see your name on the Caller ID, next to a peace sign and a heart.

It brings forth your brief and endearing appearance in last night's dream. We were walking aimlessly, stopped at a pet shop—it was in Chicago but it wasn't.

I pick up and say: Hey, got you on speaker.

I close my laptop, take a pen out from behind my ear. I say: It sounds like too good of a deal, I wouldn't buy it off this guy.

I say: All we have to do is stop!

ACKNOWLEDGMENTS

I cannot thank Jerry Brennan and Tortoise Books enough for the unbelievable amount of care put into this book. *Stun* could not have a better home.

A version of this book served as the creative component in my doctoral thesis, "Autobiography of Ember: Exploring Narratorial Voice and Poetic Form in Stories of Addiction, Trauma, and Coming of Age." A special thanks to my supervisors and first readers, Stephen Mooney and Beth Palmer, who provided invaluable feedback piece by piece. Thank you also to the University of Surrey and my examiners: Bran Nicol, Tim Atkins, Carl Thompson, and Angela Szczepaniak.

Thank you to the Creative Writing programs at DePaul University and The New School, and the mentorship, encouragement, and writing philosophy of Laurie Sheck that made this book possible.

The name of the drug was inspired by the award-winning E4 British drama *Skins* (2007-2013), where two characters in Series 3, Episode 7 are given a tablet carton labeled STUN. The doctors guaranteed it would help them "calm down" and "tell the truth." But viewers never saw or heard of it again. Thank you to the creators, Bryan Elsley and Jamie Brittain.

I could not have written it without the influence of the following books: *Brave New World* by Aldous Huxley, *Autobiography of Red* by Anne Carson, *Outline of My Lover* by Douglas A. Martin, *Bluets* by Maggie Nelson, *Robinson Alone* by Kathleen Rooney, and *On Earth We're Briefly Gorgeous* by Ocean Vuong. Thank you to the authors.

Thank you to Sanna Jordansson and Conor McNeill, two of my favorite writers, for several parts of this book that were inspired by your own work and our chats.

More thanks to the following people for their incredible support: Kevin, Libby, and Ella Chapman, Lauren Niemier, Daniela Olszewska, Deanna Belos aka Sincere Engineer, George Fear, Tom Maguire, the whole Kathyrn Guelcher family, James Block, Mark Turcotte, Michelle Middleton, Chelsea Martin, Anthony Koranda, Peter Jaeger, and especially, my parents.

This book is in memory of Dan Novakowski (1960-2021).

About the Author

Becky Wills received a BA from DePaul University, an MFA from The New School, and a PhD from University of Surrey, where she teaches creative writing. She is the founder of Own Your Life Writing, a UK based not-for-profit organization offering educational tools and resources to give people the confidence, skills, and support to write their own life experiences. Originally from Chicagoland, she lives in the south of England.

About Tortoise Books

Slow and steady wins in the end, even in publishing. Tortoise Books is dedicated to finding and promoting quality authors who haven't yet found a niche in the marketplace—writers producing memorable and engaging works that will stand the test of time.

Learn more at www.tortoisebooks.com or follow us on social media:

BlueSky @tortoisebooks.bsky.social

Instagram @tortoise.books

www.ingramcontent.com/pod-product-compliance
Lightning Source LLC
Jackson TN
JSHW020248270226
98464JS00001B/2

* 9 7 8 1 9 6 5 1 9 9 2 9 9 *